An Unbeatable Strategy of Failure

Caprice Reader № 4

Cover art by Dan Thompson
fabcrew.com

Published by Caprice Books
Las Vegas, NV, U.S.A.
Copyright © Caprice Books, 2015

For information about Caprice Books, about the work
in this book, or about our contributors, you may
contact the publisher at capricebooks@gmail.com.
Reply, if any, will be slow.

An Unbeatable Strategy of Failure
Caprice Reader № 4
ISBN 978-0-9849159-0-3

Visit us on the web!
facebook.com/capricebooks
capricebooks.blogspot.com

Do not expect much.

for Barbara

Also available from
CAPRICE BOOKS

Caprice Reader #1: If it won't reach...stretch

Caprice Reader #2: Powerless Point

Caprice Reader #3: The dust NEVER settles

Television Hates Itself

This Motel is a Museum

Buy Caprice Books on

LuLu.com

CONTENTS

"Creepy First Impressions Boy"
Benjamin Miller
facebook.com/benjamin.hoponpop

Failure and Love

I work with people who know they have failed: failed their kids, if they have them; their families; themselves. I facilitate two ongoing groups for lifers (in a men's and a women's state prison) and two with short-term prisoners (men and women) in a county jail. Makes sense for me: I long thought myself a failure too.

Some tell us their failure was in getting caught: especially men in jail, because some think there's still a good chance they can go back out and succeed at their chosen profession.

That they tell us at all is pretty astonishing. But we are often trusted. I'm white and more college prof than street smart, but my co-facilitator in the jail is an African American great grandmother, one-time Panther, married to a lifer, a straight talker who quickly gets one of two responses: an unspoken no thank you ma'am, that's too deep (and we never see them again because our classes are voluntary), or listening to you can change my life, I'll be back next week.

One of her signs, printed in huge type on a single sheet of paper reads:

EXCUSES ARE THE NAILS THAT HOLD THE HOUSE OF FAILURE TOGETHER.

Another reads:

IF YOU REALLY WANT TO DO SOMETHING, YOU'LL FIND A WAY. IF YOU DON'T, YOU'LL FIND AN EXCUSE.

Some men put them on the wall by their bunks.

Some say they failed, but it wasn't their fault. It was their crimey's, for snitching on them. Or for turning a plain vanilla robbery into a homicide. They'll do better next time: that is, work alone, or choose a more dependable crimey.

We ask: who was hurt? Sometimes we are told: no one, I was only doing credit card fraud. But usually several people in the circle then say: un-huh, there are no victimless crimes; credit card fraud means other people have to pay more interest.

Sometimes men say: I never thought

about the person I robbed / hit / accidentally killed. I have just been focused on the stupidity or bad luck I had in getting in over my head / caught / shopped.

But many know exactly how much they have failed their families and themselves and are desperate to find a way not to come back to jail, or to persuade the Parole Board to let them out of prison.

For those for whom it has truly sunk in that they hurt, maimed, killed another human being, the sense of failure changes shape. A man weeps, thirty years after killing his woman. The shame seems bottomless. What do you need to heal?, we ask him.

Toxic shame and self-hate may sound like what you want a person who has murdered to feel. And indeed many lifers say that to take accountability and open your heart to feel the full dimensions of the hurt you have caused is harder than serving a prison sentence; it may be the hardest punishment of all. But take accountability and self-knowledge further and they go beyond punishment and into love: love for those you hurt and eventually for yourself too, because as we say in restorative justice it is hurt people who hurt people. Some may feel empathy for another but never for themselves: but the journey of empathy knows no walls, go with it deep enough and you find yourself mourning for your own younger self, loving that hurt person, as much as your victims.

One man says: all this talk of childhood trauma is bullshit, it's just excuses, I made bad choices. I'm bad, says another. Some lifers are so deep in their guilt and the shame that even looking at why they were so angry, so addicted, so unfeelingly vicious, so dependent on carrying the gun for courage or image, looks to them like they are making excuses; minimizing their fault; dishonoring the person they killed.

We talk about the difference between an excuse and a reason. An excuse: I was traumatized, so it wasn't my fault—my mother was an addict, my father in prison, I joined a gang to get love, I only did what I had to do to be part of it. A reason: I was traumatized and didn't know it and made poor choices; and now the more I know about why I was the way I was, the more I can see how I am still acting out of my hurts, how I can start to find the help I need to heal, give myself the compassion I need in order to go forward.

A woman who survived multiple crimes and acts of sexual abuse as a child tells us at our nonprofit's annual fundraiser that nowadays — after much healing work — all the hurt, which used to drive her to misery, has shrunk in her awareness. Now it feels like she is looking at it through her rear view mirror. It has become small enough that she can focus on the windshield and the road ahead.

We work with everyone in our groups to get to the point where they can forgive themselves for their most terrible acts and their routine failures, because you can't drive a car looking in the rear view mirror.

When I started this prison work at age 62 I had to face my own shame: that I was raised in highly privileged circumstances and taught from my mother's milk to spend my life giving to others and did precious little of it. But now I get it too. I just need to understand why, and forgive myself, and even love myself, so that I can focus on the road ahead, and on doing what I most want to do, which is to love my family and friends, and do good work in the world.

I go so far as to imagine this restorative justice movement I am part of will one day replace the punitive injustice system altogether. And learning how to do that will give us an entirely different experience of how to respond to harm everywhere —

bedroom, boardroom, war room, or planet.

Still, my loving the work doesn't require that to happen. I expect we'll fail in many ways. But every time I see someone start to love herself in spite of her failure, I am exhilarated.

-Dave Belden

*Dave is the author of the speculative fiction novels **Children of Arable** and **To Warm the Earth**, originally published by Signet, and now available on vivisphere.com and Amazon.*

Genetic
Meltdown

*Written in Baked,
Van Brunt Street, Brooklyn,
on my iPhone, Oct 8th, 2014*

As I sleepily sip my cappuccino, and look
out at the early morning figures of Red
Hook, Brooklyn, I cannot but wonder what
oddities are occurring inside me as my
genetic machinery fumbles with the sacred
text handed down through countless
speechless and unrecorded generations. The
Neanderthal inside me aches to escape from
the confines of the new and foreign
landscape that has been imposed on it by
random change. The unborn forms similarly
struggle for their own realization, and the
trees shake in confusion. Amidst this
complex situation, I sit unperturbed and
unaware of longer-term agendas that might
take my information forward, backwards,
or round in circles. I am silent on the topic
of irreversibility, and indifferent as to
whether I will fly like a bat, descend like a

sea bird, or detect visual signals, as yet unseen. I am a moment, a frozen second, a shadow, a sparkling reflection. The words of countless generations linger in the air, and the failure of their dreams goes unnoticed, while the tick-tock of mutation undermines all it encounters, turning pharaohs into dust, and transforming streetwalkers into kings. The intrinsic failure of a mechanism designed to maintain our integrity and that defines the engine generating the possibility of all future existence. Silently, and incrementally, undermining us at every moment.

-Adrian Woolfson
adrianwoolfson.com

*Adrian is the author of two critically acclaimed books on the subject of genetics, and is currently working on his latest book, **Immortality and the Art of Living Well: A New Utopia.***

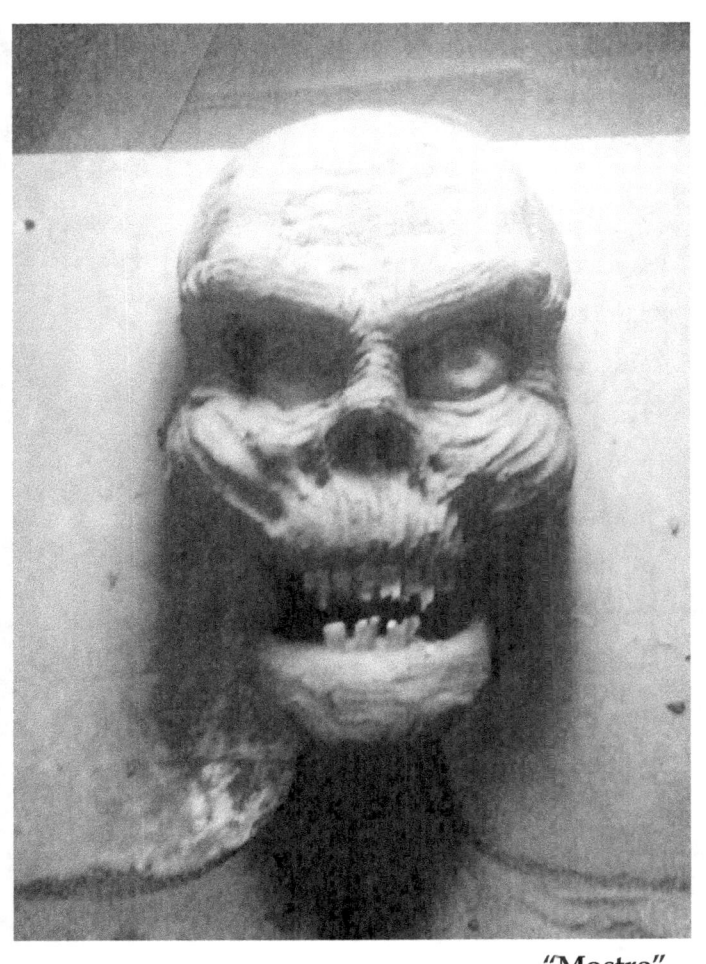

"Mostro"
*Gio*gio Guidi*
giorgicguidi.com

No Peddlers or Agents Allowed, Just Plain Ole You

We've gotten no better than
52 years gone, as if a tiered status
matters when we quake. As if
a tiered status came from the painted
index finger – male figure to male figure
The psychosis of falling for power. Eyes
never losing gluttony. Darwin
mentions love ninety-nine times. How we
all got here. Poof!   Survival
only ever comes down to feeding. We can
never win a war with such company
at the table. We will never win a heart
with vanity fisted so tightly.

-Sunnylyn Thibodeaux

The School of Intuition Has Closed Its Doors

It wasn't
without
thought
which drug
not to take
       It was
       never
       a wrap
       your arms around not your head
       gesture.   Simpletons
       Straightened finger
       banded in gold
Pay us the money
for the experiment
and maybe
we won't
talk.
Maybe Our ocean.
       Our cloud. Our take-on world swipe
       poke. Walk on
They know
the names
we go by already
DNA programmed
to fit. Franklins
waving us on

-Sunnylyn Thibodeaux

Torn at the Seams

Failure of the moon to illuminate
the creatures drooling for our crumbs
     instinctual, but far from natural
               fills us with need

Let the ghost pass us in the hall
He's paid his dues. Brutal
life sucked him dry
Hands outstretched
where no eyes would meet

This is what failure looks like, moon!
    how fellow creatures do not see the other
    as such, only ways to climb the backs of

The departed at my side
The departed at my side

          How many used him
          to hoist themselves
               bank rolls and step stools

Moon, I thought you would pelt wigs with
humility
while they pick their teeth with bones. Flashy
grill, luminous as pure. Hollowed center

Moon are you there?
The departed at my side awaits atonement
Dark sighted morning light. Digits flipping
count. Their eyes have blackened. The 1:1
ratio outweighed by voracity sponsorships
and poster children for how we need
Over time the G-R was replaced with the N
No one recognized the shift. Brainwashing
at its best.
No matter the anarchist pose or the servants
hands
Greed will somehow eat your dinner
Hoist you up on someone's something
The departed at my side awaited his bit
The departed. The departed at my side
                who never left his post

                    -*Sunnylyn Thibodeaux*

Sunnylyn is the author of several books of poetry, including **Palm to Pine** *and* **As Water Sounds** *(Bootstrap),* **88 Haiku for Lorca** *(Push Press),* **Room Service Calls** *(Lew Gallery Editions), and* **Against What Light** *(Ypolita).*

A Moral with a Story

The Moral:

Dreams very often do come true, but not always as we want.

The Story:

It was 1965 and I was teaching Latin at Park School, a private preparatory academy then located in the middle of the bucolic Marian College campus on Cold Springs Road in Indianapolis.

I had a great respect for all of my students. One student, David, was the smallest boy in my Latin II class, and I went out of my way to let him know that I valued his ideas. So one day when he suggested that we, as a class, should build and fire a catapult just like the ones Caesar had used, I encouraged him to look into it.

The next day, Andy, one of David's classmates, brought in a small plastic model of a Roman bow-powered rock-hurling machine called a ballista, and the whole class immediately became absorbed in the project. They all went to work researching typical weights and distances that Caesar's engineers might have worked with.

As a class, we decided our goal would be to build a bow-powered ballista that could hurl a 100-pound rock 100 yards.

We went to work, using only hand tools at my insistence, in order to approximate the ancient experience. The Assistant Headmaster of Park School then got the idea to notify NBC in New York of our project. To my surprise they became interested.

Pressured to give them a launch date for our catapult, I chose the Ides of March 1966 as the day our catapult, christened the Mars I, would take to the field.

When the 15th of March arrived, my students proudly rolled their recreated ancient weapon out onto the firing field, surrounded not only by the entire student body of Park School and their parents, but also by the Marian College marching band, and an NBC film crew led by Pat Trese that had flown in that morning from New York. Standing by was a motorcycle courier prepared to rush the film footage to the airport so it could be developed in flight and shown on national television that evening.

The excitement rose as our 100 lb. rock, which we named "Gaul Blaster," was loaded into the firing box, and the catapult was cocked. The Marian College marching band rolled the drums. The NBC news cameras pitapatted away.

Finally, David pulled the firing cord! Gaul Blaster tumbled from its box, rolled sadly down the front of the machine and plopped to a stop. The crowd of several hundred spectators stood dumbfounded for a moment—then broke into hilarious laughter.

Pat Trese, the NBC producer, went on to win awards with his coverage of our inadvertent comic tragedy. But my students and I were undaunted. We redesigned our machine and tried again the next year. And the next. And the next.

National news teams returned each year and our ongoing efforts were featured on the show First Tuesday in 1969 and 1970. Soon other schools joined in the experiment, including North Central High School and even Culver Military Academy.

One day, in the middle of a class, I received word from the office that I had an important phone call. To my astonishment, it was the Pentagon. Apparently the Viet Cong had been using catapults to fling logs up into the air to fowl the propellers of American helicopters. The American generals had heard of our catapult project and had decided it was time for their men to get a crash course (so to speak) in catapulting. I was told that in exchange for advising them in this matter, I could have anything we needed to aide us in our quest—engineering advice, personnel, trucks, cranes—anything.

So in 1971, emboldened by our wildly expanded mission, my students and I sponsored the First National Catapult Contest, which was featured on NBC's Chronolog.

During all this time, a machine had yet to be built by any of the participating schools that could achieve our original goal of hurling a 100 lb. rock 100 yards. This, however, didn't dampen media interest in the project. Chronolog came back again in 1972, and articles about the National Catapult Contest were published in the New York Times and Sports Illustrated.

Around this time, a young woman named Mary Hyde, a North Central H.S. Latin student, announced she was building a mammoth catapult called a trebuchet, which she had named "Zephyrus." Her status as the only female participant in our Roman catapult project caught the attention of ABC, and she was invited that year to appear on To Tell The Truth.

It ultimately took Mary three years to perfect the 6-story high Zephyrus. Then finally, on a beautiful Saturday in May 1977, during what can only be described as a pseudo-religious experience, Mary made our dreams come true. Zephyrus hurled Gaul Blaster, our original 100 lb. rock, 579 feet down field, nearly doubling our original goal.

We stood in astonishment admiring Mary's accomplishment. The official measurements were solemnly recorded in the log and then slowly, as the awe-filled moment passed, we all realized that no members of the media, local or national, were on hand.

As always news releases had been sent out to everyone who had ever covered or might want to cover the event. But after eleven years of consistent interest, that was the year everyone pulled the plug on our coverage.

Later we found out that some members of the local media had indeed intended to cover the competition, but earlier that morning the robbery and brutal murder of the Safeway heiress, Marjorie Jackson, had been committed just four blocks west of the field where our catapults were being fired, and all of the local reporters and camera crews had been re-assigned at the last minute.

The main two perpetrators charged with the Jackson crime were Howard "Billy Joe" Willard, who was convicted of murder, sentenced to life and died in prison, and Manuel Lee Robinson, who was convicted of arson and burglary and was paroled in 1988.

I can't help but think…maybe if those boys had taken Latin, things would have turned out different, for all of us.

-Bernard F. Barcio, L.H.D.

Bernard is the author of several books, including **Catapult Design, Construction & Competition**, *available on Amazon, and the memoir* **That's Not The Way I Remember It**, *available on Lulu.com.*

"Many Creeps Boy"
Benjamin Miller
facebook.com/benjamin.hoponpop

Art School Dispatch

"I never know where I am going with a painting. I only know where I've been, and frankly, I believe that every painter is in a state of constant failure."   -William Bailey

I have always loved this quote by William Bailey. It reminds me that failure is part of the painter's process and should be championed.

The images on these pages are from the painting studio where I teach. They are the marks left behind on the walls from my painting students. They are not paintings. I believe that these unintentional marks have more soul than most of the paintings the students have intentionally executed.

While teaching, I walk around taking photographs of these marks, documenting the true art happening in the room.

Every once in a while a student comments, "Wow that's cool." My response follows, "You should paint like this. It has soul, unlike what you are trying so hard to do in that painting you have been working on for weeks."

They laugh and think I'm joking. I'm not.

-Audrey Barcio

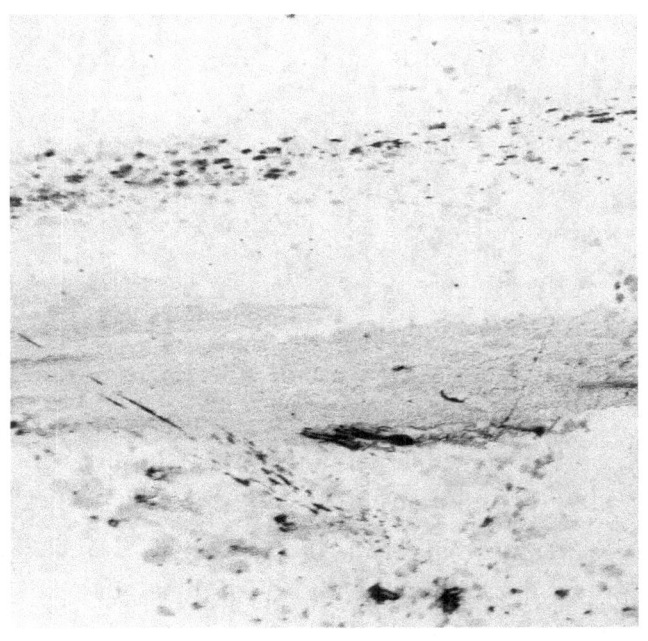

Audrey is an MFA candidate at the University of Nevada, Las Vegas, where she teaches beginning painting and drawing.

Empty Clearing

Suddenly there was a song in an empty clearing

Surrounded and protected by towering intent

And it grew and grew

And some words came and hands wrote them down

And it was sung in thoughts and quiet zum-zums,

In the shower.

On the street.

In a car.

It was alive. There were dreams about how meaningful it would be

And how people would hear it and think about it and thoughtlessly hum it,

While they baked a loaf of bread, or cut the grass or woke in the middle of the night

Thirsty for warm milk.

But it still must be trapped and captured, caught and snared ... finally locked into reality

In some kind of polymeric cage, trapped forever

In the physical world, able to be deciphered only by magnets and electricity.

For months and months

For years! It has escaped its pen

Given reprieve only by the hunter's own sleepiness, laziness

Unwillingness to pick up his rifle and aim and squeeze.

It's still there now, waiting, romping, playing on an endless loop

Living through decades, living forever

Hiding in plain sight, running through the scrubby underbrush,

staring, taunting, laughing

With a hundred of its friends.

-Sean O'Neil

*Sean lives in Indianapolis and tries to sometimes make music, do some woodworking and write words, most recently being included in **Aim For The Head: An Anthology of Zombie Poetry**, published by Write Bloody Publishing.*

The Marriage Collection Container and the Trouble with Should

Nolan's cleft palate repair was scheduled for a Friday morning in early December. No one would know by looking at him that he had a gaping hole in the roof of his mouth, because it only involved the soft tissue, not the lip or bony material close to the teeth. And the two scars tracing his tiny jaw line — reminders of a previous brush with death — were obscured until he was caught belly-laughing with his head tilted back. Even then, most people were too focused on the blue glasses, and the fat cheeks to see the story his face never stopped telling.

To prepare for Nolan's procedure, I filled a plastic bin with crowd favorites to occupy The Small One during those first few unbearable nights in the hospital. The Very Hungry Caterpillar, Baby Einstein DVDs, all the usual. I also included a couple of onesies with arm immobilizers sewn into the sleeves. All the other Cleft Palate Moms in clinic reported that toddlers were capable of all manner of sorcery when it came to getting arm immobilizers off in the night. In theory, the enhanced onesies would keep Nolan from getting his hands in his mouth post-operatively. I tried not to think about what could happen if he discovered a flaw in the design.

I developed Operation Anti-Surprise Plan, and it seemed bullet proof. Whenever I imagined our baby boy on round-the-clock narcotics, I'd check another item off The ASP. Sometimes I'd drop a soapy, warm sponge into the sink mid-dish duty to add another item to the bin.

Trying to find two square feet of clear mind space in the months leading up to this surgery became nearly impossible for me, because The Scrubs never stopped recommending. Make smoothies and freeze them. That's the only way to get enough nutrients in after surgery. Yes, he'll lose weight. They all do. He won't be allowed to suck for eight weeks, so work on open cups now. No more bottles after the repair.

Why not? Subjecting a baby to the worst pain he'd ever experienced in his short life, and then taking away his primary calming mechanism sounded like a great plan.

Anticipating Nolan's reaction to all these things, those searching blue eyes begging for comfort, made me nauseous. He never asked for any of this. We were standing on the edge of a hurricane, and the path to healing demanded we walk right into the center of it. This whole situation required a level of resolve I didn't really possess. But, by the night before his surgery, I'd arrived at a place of broken readiness months in the making.

And that's the night he threw up all over the place.

I got the call while I was out having dinner with my sister. All the months of planning, all the psychological and emotional rallying, everything, now lay buried in a river of toddler vomit. When I got home, I ventured down to the basement, surveyed the coffin of frozen food I'd prepared in advance, and then trudged back up the stairs in disillusionment.

I made the confessional call to the surgery center. That was that. The surgeon's schedule is pretty tight, so the new date will probably be a month or two out. No problem.

The next day, I stayed in bed until noon. I might have cried a little, too. Considering all that could have been didn't help my mood. With a shiny, new palate, food would no longer shoot out Nolan's nose after every meal — which meant the sinus infections would slow down. He could finally start speech therapy. The negative pressure needed to make sounds like, "puh" and "kuh" would finally be possible. With an anatomically correct oral cavity, Nolan could wrestle a twenty-foot python and win.

I decided to temper my disappointment with helpful self-talk, like: Really, Meredith? How many times do we have to circle this wagon? You don't run the show around here. You never have. Psyching myself up all over again for this thing called for reinforcement.

The day after Nolan's missed surgery, I turned to the coping strategy of choice. One

I hadn't done in over a year: hot yoga.

Sweating out my demons always improved my outlook on life. After the year I'd spent away from yoga, I was ready for an exorcism. I suited up: sports bra (fitting slightly snugger than I remembered), yoga pants, mat, towel, and three thousand gallons of water.

As I walked out the door, I saw something shiny on the kitchen counter. The gleam of my wedding bands. After having Nolan, my ring size, like the rest of me...evolved. Fourteen months later, I still hadn't gotten around to buying new clothes or getting the bands resized.

And then, it happened.

You really should wear those rings, Meredith. How do you think Grant feels when he comes downstairs to make himself a Paleo smoothie and sees the way you've cast aside those priceless tokens of his love?

Feeling optimistic, I forced the rings onto my finger. They "fit." A Christmas miracle!

I swung my yoga mat over my shoulder and smiled to myself. I was a good wife, after all.

Hot yoga did what hot yoga always does for me. I came home energized, exorcized and ready for round two. That night, I fell into bed, satisfied and happy.

At five o'clock in the morning, my whole body woke up all at once. My attention shot over to my left hand, where my wedding bands cinched my ring finger like a tourniquet.

I tried in vain for over an hour to remove the bands of blasphemy, using all the YouTube strategies I could attempt without involving another person.

Rational thoughts subjected themselves to the authority of the Primitive Brain. By now, the sirens going off in my head refused to be ignored. I woke and briefed Grant on the events of the past hour or so, told him I was going to the ER, and dressed myself. I backed out of our driveway around six thirty, wearing a pair of three day-old jeans, a stained Food Allergy Awareness T-shirt from 2009, a frumpy black hoodie, and what I thought was a matching pair of clogs. I drove off into the darkness, hoping there wouldn't be a long wait at the emergency room.

Under the fluorescent glow of the ER parking lot, I learned an important lesson in buying two identical pairs of shoes in different colors.

My recall of lobby events is patchy, at best. What with all the adrenaline and primal fear hormones coursing through my body, few details survived. I said hello to the receptionist. I asked for a nurse to come up front and determine if check-in would be necessary, or if a locked psych unit might be a better fit.

A few minutes later, a nurse materialized.

"Do I even need to be here?" I asked, holding up my hand.

"Did you hit your hand on something?" she asked, taking my hand in hers and trying to rotate the ring on my finger. It wouldn't budge. Maybe her scrubs were sapphire blue. That sounds right.

"Nope." I replied with a blank, unintelligent stare. I'm pretty sure her hair was straight. Chin-length, blonde. "I just woke up a few hours ago and it was stuck." I straightened the neckline of my Food Allergy Awareness T-shirt and tried to hide the black shoe by standing on it with the brown one.

"Come on back," said the faceless Nurse. I walked in the trail of her Estee Lauder perfume, thinking about the peculiarity of being on the receiving end of medicine. I decided not to tell them that I'm an occupational therapist—especially since I presented more like a woman off her meds than a medical professional with fifteen years of experience. I tried hard not to think about my shoes.

We walked toward the exam room. The familiar smell of industrial cleaning products and packaged medical supplies, settled into my bones. No Name Nurse handed my off to Janet.

Janet's laugh-less, cynical nurse tone immediately put me at ease for four whole seconds. This one knew how to prevent my finger from spontaneously amputating like some sort of lizard's tail.

Thirty-minute wait, then Dr. Bloom entered the room. Young face. Clean-shaven. Bald and completely approachable. I pointed to my shoes and smiled.

"Nice," he grinned.

I held up my hand. "Am I crazy for being here?"

"Oh no…" he replied, "those are gonna have to come off today. Have you ever heard of compartment syndrome?"

Excessive pressure building up in an enclosed space. Affirmative.

Just as a wave of validation was about to wash over me, a new challenge emerged. Everyone seemed really interested in saving the rings. Not cutting them off.

"I'm just going to throw this out there,"

I offered, checking the urge to be inappropriate. "If you need to cut these off, I promise not to get all emotional."

"Oh no!" Dr. Bloom replied, aghast that I'd even suggested it. "We have our ways. We only cut off wedding bands when we absolutely have to."

Why did all these fine people insist on superimposing their sentimentality on me, while the life force was draining out of my finger? Cut them off. Do it now.

Eventually they figured out what I already knew. All the YouTube videos in the world couldn't save my rings. KY jelly, string, a small piece of tourniquet to make a sort of Spanx girdle over which my rings should have effortlessly glided. Each new strategy to free my finger resulted in more swelling. My heart rate was somewhere in the 120's by the time the medical staff saw things in a proper light.

It took Dr. Bloom minutes to cut my rings. He frowned, placing the broken symbols of the past seven years in my hand.

"Do you guys have anything I can put these in?" I asked. "So I don't lose them?"

Janet looked at me over her gold-rimmed glasses. "Not really," she said in that matter-of-fact nurse tone, "but I'll go look in the supply room." I didn't think anyone younger than my grandmother still believed in the perm, but it fit her somehow.

She came back and handed me a urine collection container.

I signed the papers, and thanked everyone.

I hadn't banged my finger with a hammer or slammed it in a door. The trouble started with should.

Hot yoga, the chaturangas, the down dogs, the warmth of the room and the pressure distributed through my hands with each pose. All would have been well, had I left my rings on the counter where they belonged.

The thin band of red blisters around the fourth digit of my left hand throbbed and pulsed, and I pushed the Marriage Collection Container deep into the folds of my purse.

-Francie Taylor

Francie Taylor is a writer and artist living in Fishers, Indiana, and a frequent contributor to the Caprice Reader.

Caprice Reader #4:
An Unbeatable Strategy
of Failure

www.ingramcontent.com/pod-product-compliance
Lightning Source LLC
Chambersburg PA
CBHW061502170626
46811CB00004B/1598